W9-AFD-821

The Quiet Farmer

By Marni McGee

Illustrated by Lynne Dennis

Atheneum   1991   New York

Collier Macmillan Canada · Toronto
Maxwell Macmillan International Publishing Group
New York · Oxford · Singapore · Sydney

To Elizabeth, with love, and in memory
of the quiet farmer, William Earl Broach
                       —M. M.

For Baby Drew   *—L. D.*

Atheneum, Macmillan Publishing Company, 866 Third Avenue, New York, NY 10022. Collier Macmillan Canada, Inc., 1200 Eglinton Avenue East, Suite 200, Don Mills, Ontario M3C 3N1. First edition. Printed in Hong Kong by South China Printing Company (1988) Ltd. 1 2 3 4 5 6 7 8 9 10

Library of Congress Cataloging-in-Publication Data. McGee, Marni. The quiet farmer/by Marni McGee: illustrated by Lynne Dennis.—1st ed. p. cm. Summary: From sunup to sundown, the quiet farmer hears many different types of sounds. ISBN 0–689–31678–x [1. Sound—Fiction. 2. Farm life—Fiction.] I. Dennis, Lynne, ill. II. Title. PZ7.M478463Qu 1991 [E]—dc20 90-37930

In a pocket of earth between two hills,
a quiet farmer lives alone far from the sounds of town.

And when in the morning the sun first appears,
the rooster begins to crow.
Cock-a-doo, cock-a-doo. Cock-a-doodle-doo!

Hearing the rooster's bugle call,
the quiet farmer opens his eyes.
He stretches and gets out of bed.
Squeak go the bedsprings.
Creak goes the floor.

The yellow cat begins to purr.
Purr-purr.
The quiet farmer kneels.
He picks her up and holds her close.

The farmer knows there's work to do.
He dresses and goes outside.
And as he walks down to the barn,
a pail bumps at his knee.
Bong, bong, boink.
Bong, bong, boink.

Moo-moo, Old Bessie says.
The quiet farmer sits.
Spling-splosh goes the milk
up to the top of the pail.
The farmer fills a little bowl
to give to the yellow cat.
Lip-lap, lip-lap, lip-lap.
The farmer rubs Old Bessie's neck.

Next the chickens must be fed.
Puck-puck, puckety-puck.
The quiet farmer gathers eggs
and puts them in a basket.

The horses in the stable snort.
Snee-snort, snee-snort.
They stamp their hooves
to ask for grain.
Thump-thump. Thumpity-thump.
The quiet farmer feeds them all.

Now that his friends have all been fed,
the quiet farmer feeds himself.
The kitchen sings a breakfast song.
Gurgle goes the coffee pot.
The frying pan says, *Sizzle!*
And the porridge kettle
on top of the stove says,
Bubble-de-blip, bubble-de-blop.

With breakfast done,
it's back to work—
the quiet farmer goes to the field
and sets the tractor roaring.
Vroom-vroom-vroom!!

The quiet farmer plows
and then he scatters seed.
Soo-swish, soo-swish, soo-swish.
All through the day, the farmer works.
He hoes. *Scritch-scratch.*
He mows. *Clack-clack.*

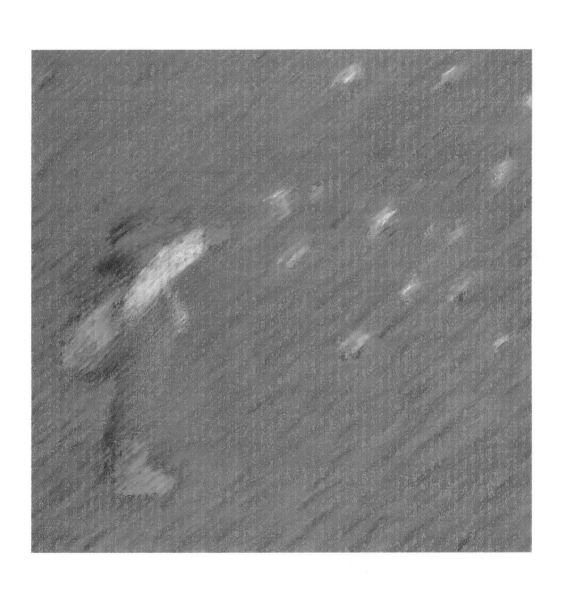

At dusk the farmer feeds his pigs.
Oink-oink, squeal-squoink.
They squish and squash in barnyard mud.
The quiet farmer mops his brow,
decides his work is done.

But then he sees
the fence needs mending.
He takes his tools
and nails the boards in place—
Whop-whop-bang.
Whop-whop-bang!

When all his chores are finally done,
the quiet farmer sits
to rest and rock out on the porch
and hear the crickets sing.
The farm is in shadow, yet lit by stars
and the tiny flares of lightning bugs.
Eerk goes the rocking chair.
The crickets answer, *chuzzit, chuzzit.*

At last the farmer speaks with words.
"Goodnight," he says. "Goodnight
to my rooster, my cat, and my cow.
Goodnight to the stars,
the wind, and the plow.
Goodnight, goodnight—
it's time to sleep now."

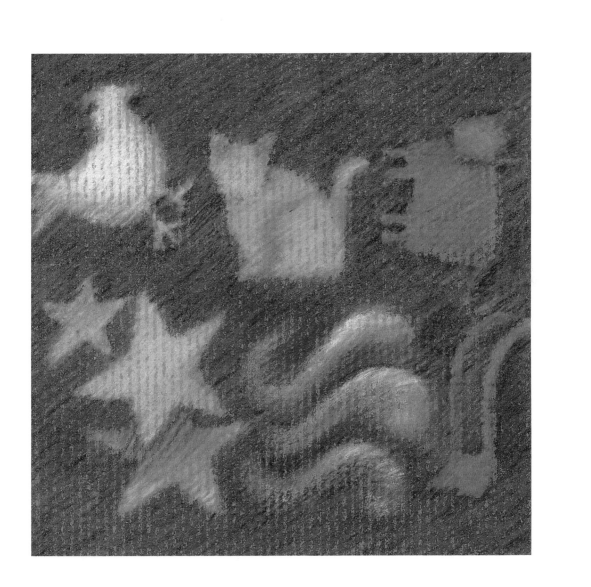

The quiet farmer goes upstairs.
He puts on his nightshirt—
gets ready for bed.
Creak goes the floor.
Squeak go the bedsprings.
The farmer crawls under the covers
and pulls them up to his chin.
The moon shines through the window,
casting a silver glow.

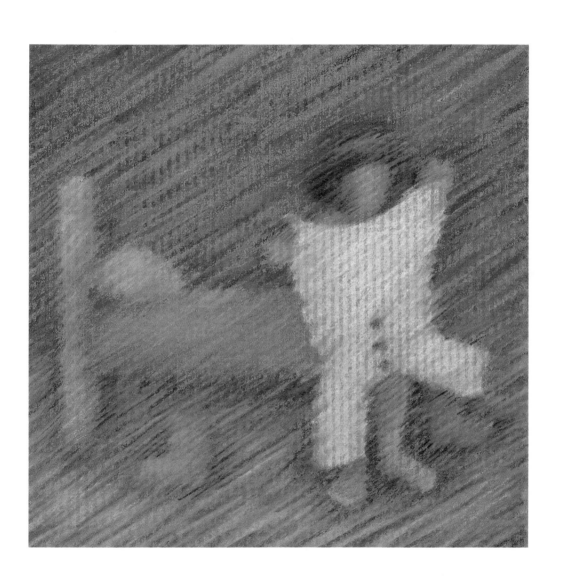

The yellow cat
is curled like a C
at the foot of the farmer's bed.
Purr-purr.

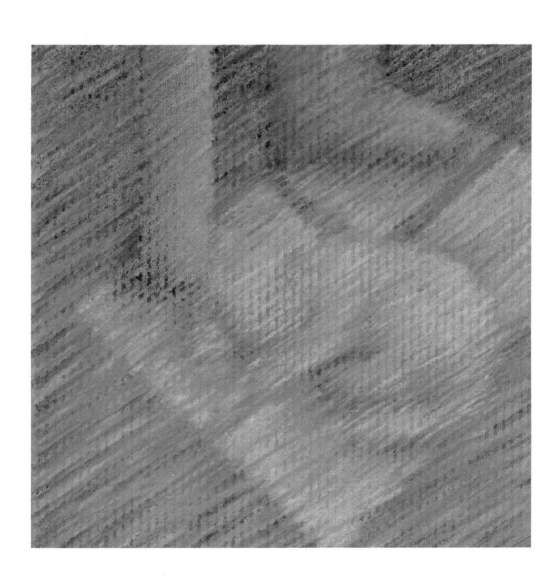

Outside an owl is calling,
Whooo-whooo-whoooo.
But the farmer does not answer.
His eyes are closed.
His breath is deep.
The quiet farmer is fast asleep.